GRANPA

John Burningham

Dragonfly Books
CROWN PUBLISHERS, INC. • *New York*

Other books by John Burningham

Where's Julius?

*John Patrick Norman McHennessy
—the boy who was always late*

*Humbert, Mister Firkin and the
Lord Mayor of London*

Hey! Get Off Our Train

Aldo

A DRAGONFLY BOOK PUBLISHED BY
CROWN PUBLISHERS, INC.

Published in the United States in 1985 by Crown Publishers, Inc., a Random
House company, 201 East 50th Street, New York, New York 10022

Originally published in Great Britain by Jonathan Cape Limited.
CROWN is a trademark of Crown Publishers, Inc.
Manufactured in the United States of America
Library of Congress Cataloging in Publication Data
Burningham, John.
Granpa.
Summary: A little girl and her grandfather share very special moments.
1. Children's stories, English. [1. Grandfathers—Fiction]   I. Title.
PZ7.B936Gr 1984   [E]   84-17464
ISBN: 0-517-55643-X (trade)   10 9 8 7 6 5 4 3
0-517-58797-1 (pbk.)   10 9 8 7 6 5 4 3

First Dragonfly Books edition: January 1992

And how's my little girl?

There will not be room for all the little seeds to grow.

Do worms go to Heaven?

Row row row your boat
gently down the stream...

*Little ducks, soup and sheep, sunshine in
the trees...*

I didn't know Teddy was another
little girl.

Noah knew that the ark was not far from land when he saw the dove carrying the olive branch.

Could we float away in this house, Granpa?

That was not a nice thing

to say to Granpa.

This is lovely chocolate ice cream.

It's not chocolate. It's strawberry!

When we get to the beach can we stay there forever?

Yes, but we must go back for our tea at four o'clock.

When I've finished this lollipop can we get some more? I need the sticks to make things.

When I was a boy we used to roll our
wooden hoops down the street
after school.

Were you once a baby as well, Granpa?

If I catch a fish we can cook it for supper.

What if you catch a whale, Granpa?

Harry, Florence and I used to come
down that hill like little arrows.
I remember one Christmas…

You nearly slipped then, Granpa.

Granpa can't come out to play today.

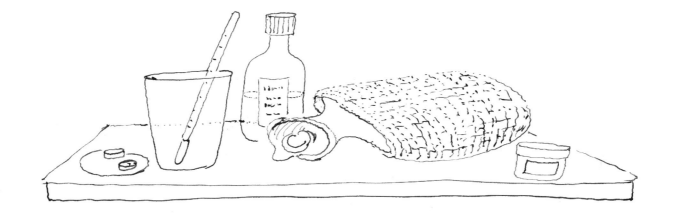

Tomorrow shall we go to Africa, and you can be the captain?